Merci à Lucie et Michel — C.A.
For Sonya — A.C.

Text © 2020 Caroline Adderson | Illustrations © 2020 Alice Carter

Owlkids Books acknowledges the financial support of the Canada Council for the Arts, the Ontario Arts Council, the Government of Canada through the Canada Book Fund (CBF), and the Government of Ontario through the Ontario Creates Book Initiative for our publishing activities.

Published in Canada by
Owlkids Books Inc.
1 Eglinton Avenue East
Toronto, ON M4P 3A1

Published in the United States by
Owlkids Books Inc.
1700 Fourth Street
Berkeley, CA 94710

Catalogage avant publication de Bibliothèque et Archives Canada

Titre: Pierre & Paul : avalanche! / Caroline Adderson ; illustrations, Alice Carter.
Autres titres: Pierre et Paul
Noms: Adderson, Caroline, 1963- auteur. | Carter, Alice, 1977- illustrateur. | Adderson, Caroline, 1963- Pierre & Paul. | Adderson, Caroline, 1963- Pierre & Paul. Français.
Description: Texte en anglais et en français.
Identifiants: Canadiana 20190149590F | ISBN 9781771473279 (couverture rigide)
Classification: LCC PS8551.D3267 P54 2020 | CDD jC813/.54—dc23

Library and Archives Canada Cataloguing in Publication

Title: Pierre & Paul : avalanche! / Caroline Adderson ; illustrations, Alice Carter.
Other titles: Pierre and Paul
Names: Adderson, Caroline, 1963- author. | Carter, Alice, illustrator. | Adderson, Caroline, 1963- Pierre & Paul. | Adderson, Caroline, 1963- Pierre & Paul. French.
Description: Text in English and French.
Identifiers: Canadiana 20190149590E | ISBN 9781771473279 (hardcover)
Classification: LCC PS8551.D3267 P54 2020 | DDC jC813/.54

Library of Congress Control Number: 2019947230

Edited by Karen Li | Designed by Jill Monsod

Manufactured in Guangdong, Dongguan, China, in October 2019 by Toppan Leefung Packaging & Printing (Dongguan) Co., Ltd.   Job #BAYDC70

A   B   C   D   E   F

Publisher of Chirp, Chickadee and OWL
www.owlkidsbooks.com | Owlkids Books is a division of bayard canada

PIERRE & PAUL

AVALANCHE!

A story told in two languages
Une histoire racontée en deux langues

WRITTEN BY/TEXTE DE
CAROLINE ADDERSON

ILLUSTRATED BY/ILLUSTRÉ PAR
ALICE CARTER

OWLKIDS BOOKS

Paul and Pierre are great explorers.

Ils sont aussi des amis.

Friends and explorers.

Today they are climbing the Himalayas.

« Quelle grande montagne ! »

"I'm hungry!" Paul shouts.

« Tu as faim ? demande Pierre. As-tu une collation ? »

"No!"

boots
bottes ☑

water ☑
eau

snacks ☐
collation

rope
corde ☑

sunscreen
crème solaire ☑

Explorers should always bring snacks.

Ils descendent de la montagne.

« Qu'est-ce que tu veux manger ? » demande Pierre.

"Anything but salad," Paul says. "I don't like salad."

« Faisons un bon sandwich, » dit Pierre.

« Quelle sorte de sandwich ? » demande Pierre à Paul.

"Let's see what you have."

Ham, cheese, mayonnaise.
Du beurre, de la laitue, un concombre.

MAYO

"We forgot the most important thing," Paul says.

« Le pain ! »

"The bread!"

Paul étale le beurre. Pierre spreads the mayonnaise.

Du jambon. Du fromage. Lettuce. Cucumber.

« C'est ennuyant, » dit Pierre.

"Really boring," Paul says. "This isn't a sandwich for explorers."

Ils regardent dans le frigo une autre fois.

Des olives. Des cornichons.

"But now it will be too salty," Paul says.

«Trop salé? Ajoutons de la confiture!

Aussi des tomates!»

« Mais il manque quelque chose, n'est-ce pas ? »
demande Pierre.

"Yes, there's something missing," says Paul.

jujubes

nourriture pour chats
cat food

vers
worms

couscous . . .

sauce piquante
hot sauce

« Du couscous ! »

They have to cook the couscous first. Pierre's mom offers to help.

« Qu'est-ce que vous faites ? elle demande.

– Un bon sandwich, répond Pierre.

– C'est bizarre! Bizarre et un peu dangereux.

– Dangereux ?» Paul asks.

Hooray! Explorers love danger!

When the couscous is ready, they pack it on, but now the sandwich is squishy.

« C'est trop spongieux. »

"Cereal!" Paul decides. "To make it crunchy."

« Fini ! dit Pierre. Ajoutons le pain ! »

The sandwich is as tall as a mountain.
A wobbly mountain!

« Oh, non ! s'écrie Pierre. C'est trop gros ! »

Et puis . . . quelle catastrophe !
Une avalanche !

Ham and fromage.

Laitue et cucumber.

Couscous and tomates.

Olives et pickles.

Cornflakes and confiture.

They all spill across the counter.

"My sandwich!" Paul cries.

« Ça ne fait rien, dit Pierre. Il prend un grand bol. Voilà ! »

"That's not a sandwich," Paul says.
"It's a salad. I don't like salad."

« Les explorateurs doivent être braves. »

« C'est pas si mal, » dit Pierre.

"Delicious!" says Paul.

« Et l'Himalaya ? demande Pierre. On y va ! »